☆ ☆ ☆ ☆ ☆

A CHRISTMAS GIFT FOR MAMA

☆ ☆ ☆ ☆ ☆

A Christm for N

for

SCHOLASTIC PRESS/NEW YORK

BY LAUREN THOMPSON

ILLUSTRATED BY JIM BURKE

To Robert—L. T.

☆　☆　☆　☆　☆

This book is dedicated to Gram,
the best Grandmother in the world. I love you.—J. B.

Text copyright © 2003 by Lauren Thompson
Illustrations copyright © 2003 Jim Burke

Library of Congress Cataloging—in—Publication Data
Thompson, Lauren.
A Christmas gift for Mama / by Lauren Thompson, illustrated by Jim Burke. — 1st ed.
p.　cm.
Summary: On the first Christmas since her father died, Grace and her mother try
to create a happy celebration through the special gifts they give each other.
ISBN 0=590=30725=8 (alk. paper)
[1. Christmas—Fiction. 2. Mothers and daughters—Fiction. 3. Dolls—Ficton.
4. Single=parent families—Fiction.] I. Burke, Jim, ill. II. Title.
PZ7.T37163Ch 2003　[E]dc—21　2002042804
10 9 8 7 6 5 4 3 2 1　03 04 05 06 07
Printed in Singapore　46
First edition, October 2003
The paintings were done in oil with some colored
pencil on Strathmore bristol board.
The display type was hand=lettered by David Coulson
The text type was set in 17=point Kuenstler 165 BT
Book design by Kristina Albertson

A VERY SPECIAL THANKS TO LAUREN THOMPSON FOR WRITING SUCH A WONDERFUL STORY, AND ALSO TO THE FOLLOWING PEOPLE WHO HELPED MAKE THIS BOOK POSSIBLE: DAVID SAYLOR, SHAUGHNESSY MILLER, SEAN AND KAREN MILLER, NANCY BELL, SUZANNE ELDER, MRS. PILLEY, ROSWITHA FULLER, MIKE STOFFER, MARIE "GRAM" BURKE, CHRIS HAWLEY, LIZ SZABLA, ZACHARY ADAMS, MARIJKA KOSTIW, FRANK CROSKY, ANNE BELLIS, CLAIRE CORBETT, KRISTINA ALBERTSON, JESSICA DIFFIE, STERLING HUNDLEY, MARY WHEELER, AND KAREN WINNEY. AND ALSO TO ROSWITHA'S COLLECTIBLE DOLLS IN AMHERST, NEW HAMPSHIRE; TOY AND MINIATURE MUSEUM OF KANSAS CITY, MISSOURI; AND THE PIANO MAN MUSIC CENTER IN MISSION, KANSAS.—J. B.

WINTER HAD COME EARLY IN THE CITY

and by the time Christmas week arrived, it seemed as if the cold wind had blown for a year. At night, to keep warm, Grace and her mother spread their coats over the worn coverlet on their one narrow bed. Ever since Papa had died the spring before, times had been hard, but now they seemed harder than ever.

Grace woke early one morning, just a few days before Christmas. She lay in bed beside her mother, huddling close to her warmth and listening to the stillness. Soon would come the sounds from the other apartments around them, the coughing of the woman downstairs, the crying of the baby down the hall, and the creaks and thuds of a crowded old building waking. But for now, except for the clatter of the passing milk truck, all was still. Grace uncurled herself from beside Mama's sleeping warmth and slipped out of bed.

Quietly Grace pulled on her one dress and a pair of long stockings. Then she tiptoed toward the kitchen, stopping, as she did every morning, before her doll, sitting among a few hairpins on the dresser top. "Good morning, Penny," Grace

"Good morning, Penny," Grace whispered.

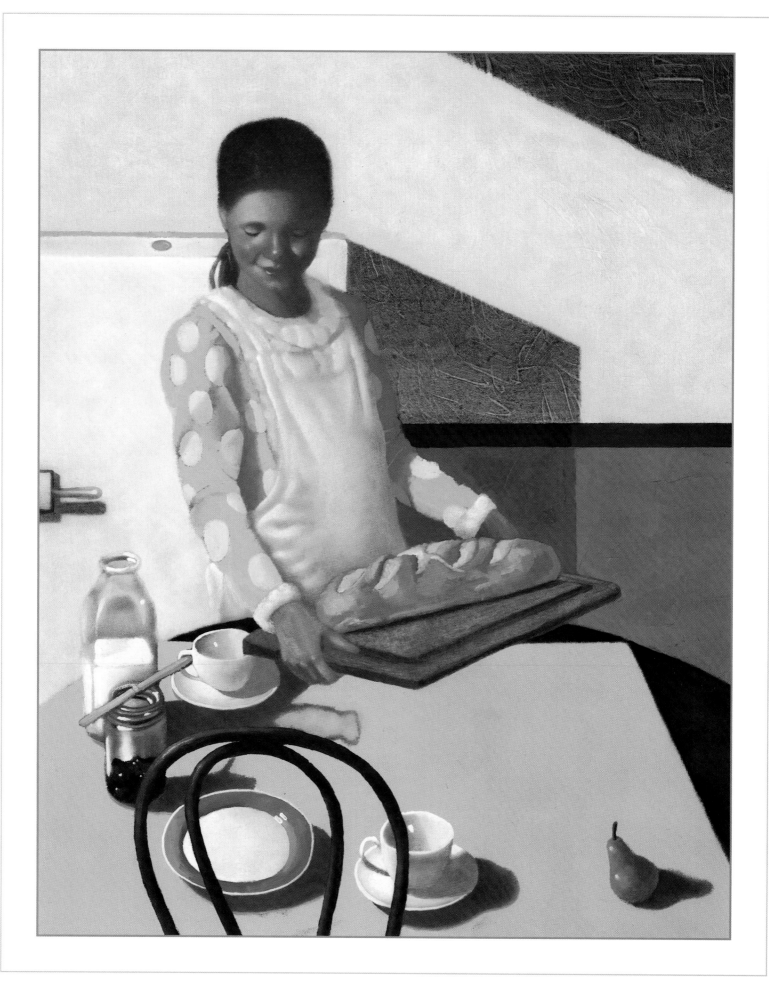

whispered. She smoothed the doll's long curls, which were coppery red like her own. She gazed into Penny's clear eyes and saw the same warm shimmer she had seen when Mama and Papa had given the doll to her, years before when she had first gone off to boarding school. Grace had always tried to take care of Penny, wiping clean her porcelain face and hands, and mending her lacy white dress as best she could. Penny had always been kind of a friend to Grace, cheering her heart when she was lonely for Mama and Papa. Now with Papa gone and Mama always so tired and sad, and so many of their familiar things sold or traded away, Penny was more of a comfort to Grace than ever, as much as a doll could be.

Grace lit the stove and filled the kettle. She would make some toast and tea. If Grace made some breakfast, she knew Mama might eat before she went to work. Otherwise there would be none, and Mama might not eat till supper. But it was not hard to make toast and tea. She would put out some butter as well as jam, since it was almost Christmas.

As Grace sliced the bread loaf with a knife, she hummed her favorite Christmas song, "We Three Kings." She thought of an evening just a year before, the evening

If Grace made breakfast, Mama might eat before work.

of their Christmas party. The house had been filled with music and laughter. Ladies in their fine, fluttering gowns and gentlemen in their elegant, black evening suits talked of their traveling and visiting. Grace wanted to stay near Mama and Papa and have them to herself, to hear Papa tell the funny stories he saved just for her, and to hear Mama's bright laughter. But with every new guest, they were called away. So Grace wandered in her own lovely dress among all the people, smiling and nod=ding though she hardly knew any of them. But then she heard Mama calling for her—"Grace? Where is our Grace?" She hurried to Mama and Papa's side near the piano, and they drew her to them. "I'm happiest when we are together," said Papa. "That's all we need to be happy, isn't it?"

"Yes, Papa," Grace answered, taking his hand.

"That's all we need," Mama said, smiling. Then Papa sat on the bench before the piano, and together Grace, Mama, and Papa sang Christmas carols for everyone. They began with "We Three Kings." "WE THREE KINGS OF ORIENT ARE, BEARING GIFTS, WE TRAVERSE AFAR," they sang. To Grace, the song had never sounded more beautiful.

Together, Grace, Mama, and Papa sang carols for everyone.

The party went on many hours, late into the evening. Though Grace had been getting tired, she stayed downstairs in hopes of seeing the dancing. But at last Mama told Grace it was time for her to go upstairs to bed.

"Next year, you may stay up as late as you like," Mama had said, kissing her on her forehead. "That's a promise."

"Next year, you may even dance!" Papa had said, taking her hands and lead= ing her through a few steps. Then he brought her hands together, kissed them, and smiled. "But not tonight."

"All right," Grace had said, laughing. She hugged them both and went upstairs.

Later, just as her eyes had closed, Grace heard the music change downstairs. The dancing had begun! Grace jumped out of bed and crept halfway down the stairs. From her perch behind the banister, she could peer into the parlor. The musicians were playing Mama and Papa's favorite dance music, the "Blue Danube Waltz." Grace saw other couples go by. Then, Mama and Papa came into view. Lightly, elegantly, they stepped and turned together. Mama was smiling serenely, her steps

Grace would never forget how lovely they looked.

so graceful she seemed to float across the floor as Papa's arms tipped ever so slightly back and forth. How lovely they had looked that night!

Not many days after, Papa had fallen ill with fever. Doctors came to the house every day, but Papa only got worse. Mama and Grace stayed by Papa's bedside day and night. For Grace, it was almost unbearable to watch her dear Papa grow weaker and weaker. But for his sake she tried to seem strong.

Grace would never forget the last thing Papa had said to her. He had whispered, "Whatever happens, Grace, take good care of Mama for me." And Grace had promised that she would.

After Papa died, everything in Mama and Grace's life suddenly changed. There were debts to be paid, large debts that Mama had not known about. The piano, the furniture, and even the house were sold so that the debts could be cleared. Grace did not return to the boarding school. Instead, Mama found them an apartment in the city, and Grace attended the dusty, crowded school a few streets away. Mama found a job at a dress shop, where she helped ladies try on dresses. The job did not pay very much, and at the end of the day, Mama's feet were sore and her shoulders ached. Though she had never sewn, Mama was trying to learn from the seamstress how to do fitting work, so that she could earn extra money. But the lessons were not going well. Mama tried to hide it from Grace, but Grace knew that Mama sometimes despaired that things would ever be good for them again. But at least she and Mama were together every day, Grace thought now as she set the table. Surely that was one way their lives were better.

Grace heard the woman downstairs begin to cough. Soon it would be time for Grace to leave for school. When the water had boiled in the kettle and the bread was toasting in the oven, Grace went into the bedroom.

Grace gently shook her mother's shoulder. "Wake up, Mama," Grace said softly. "The tea is almost ready."

"All right," Mama murmured. "I'll be there in a moment."

Grace left Mama to dress alone. She knew Mama was ashamed of the holes in her stockings and the frayed edges of her once fine clothes. She felt it was best not to let Mama know she saw these things.

As Grace closed the bedroom door, something of Mama's caught her eye on a shelf between two windows in the sitting room. It was a china figurine of a lady, dancing and swirling in a coral pink dress with gold=painted roses. There had been a china gentleman, too, elegantly dressed in high boots and a coat with a dozen glinting buttons. Papa had given them to Mama just before they were married, and Mama had always cherished them.

But the china gentleman was gone now. Grace carefully took the china lady from the shelf and remembered the day her china partner had broken.

They had been moving into this apartment, unpacking the small trunk that now held their belongings. Mama first unwrapped the china lady and put her safely to the side. Then she unrolled the rag that wrapped the gentleman. Suddenly Mama gasped. The china gentleman was in pieces. Mama tried to fit the shattered bits together again, but it was no use.

Mama pushed all the pieces into a pile and covered them with her hands. Then she bowed her head, and Grace saw her shoulders shake. She knew that Mama was crying. Grace put her arms around Mama's shoulders. "Oh, Mama," she whispered. After a moment, Mama squeezed one of Grace's hands. Then Mama quickly folded the shards into the rag and gently placed the bundle at the bottom of the dust bin. Then she went back to the unpacking.

Grace had held back her tears as she helped Mama put the rest of the things away. But later, when Mama was making up the bed, she went to the china lady and carefully held her in her hands. Then Grace wept. It had been so hard to think that the china lady would forever dance alone.

Mama was still in the bedroom now. Grace ran her fingers across the undulat=

ing folds of the china lady's skirt and smiled. She was still so lovely in her swinging

gown. Quietly, Grace began to hum a melody from the "Blue Danube Waltz."

Holding the figurine before her, Grace danced around the room. She imagined she

was wearing a beautiful, swinging gown like the china lady's.

Suddenly, the bedroom door opened. Grace stopped.

"What are you doing?" Mama asked.

"Nothing, Mama, I . . ." Grace began.

"Please put it back." Mama spoke in an urgent voice. "I want that kept safe."

"I'm sorry, Mama," Grace said. She put the china lady back on her shelf. "I've

made breakfast for us." Grace went to put the toast on the table.

Then Mama called to her gently. "Forgive me, Grace," she said, taking her

hands. "I don't mean to be harsh. I'm just so tired."

"It's all right," Grace said.

"I want things to be better for you," Mama said, "for both of us."

"It's all right, Mama," said Grace.

Grace imagined she was wearing a beautiful, swinging gown.

"You know, I'd like this Christmas to be special," Mama said. "I'd like it to be." She looked at Grace with a little smile that made her hope the better days were near.

"I'd like that, too," said Grace.

They said little as they ate their small breakfast. Grace wondered if Mama would ever be as happy as she had been last year at Christmastime. But Grace would keep her promise to Papa. She would take care of Mama till Mama could take care of the both of them again.

If there was one thing Grace wanted for Christmas, it was for Mama to be happy again.

☆　　☆　　☆　　☆　　☆

That day after school, Grace walked with some of her friends. There was a curio shop near the school, and as they often did, the girls stopped to look into the picture window.

"I've always wanted a tiny tea set like that," said Jenny.

"Look at that hat! That's elegant!" said Francie, pressing her finger on the glass before a neatly brimmed velvet hat with a long feather.

"You mean it WAS elegant," said Millicent, "before the feather got snapped."

"It's still elegant," said Grace, smiling past Millicent at Francie.

The girls stood together for another moment, silently gazing into the window, for a time not feeling the cold through their thin coats. Just when they were about to move on, something caught Grace's eye. There, on the bottom, near a jumbled col= lection of painted thimbles, was a china gentleman. It looked just like the one Papa had given Mama. But this china gentleman was not broken.

All the girls but Grace walked away, talking and laughing again. "I'll see you tomorrow," Grace called. Then she gazed once more at the figurine. Just the sight of it made her feel warm inside, as if Papa were standing right beside her, holding her hand in his. If only Mama could see the china gentleman. If only Grace could give him to Mama for Christmas!

Grace went to the door of the shop. A sign hanging inside the door window read, "Valuables Bought and Sold." Grace opened the door and stepped into the shop. "No children!" a sharp voice snapped. A small, frowning woman stood behind a counter in the corner. "No children allowed in my shop."

The girls gazed into the window, for a time not feeling the cold.

"But the china gentleman," Grace said.

"What gentleman?" the woman asked.

"The china gentleman in the window," Grace said. "How much is he?"

"Oh, the figurine," the woman grumbled. "That's not a toy, now. It came from a fine house."

"Please," said Grace, "will you tell me how much he costs?"

The woman came out from behind her counter. She reached between the wheels of a baby carriage and retrieved the dancing figurine from the window display.

"This is a nice piece," she said, wiping it with a cloth. "That's real gold on the buttons. The last owner bargained hard when she sold it to me. I couldn't sell it to you for less than five dollars."

"Five dollars!" Grace cried. Five dollars was a fortune.

"And no less," the woman said. "If you haven't got that much, then you'd better leave."

Grace thought for a moment. Grace had less than a dollar of her own money. Then she remembered how at times Mama had traded things for rent or a grocer's bill. It was worth a try now.

"No children allowed in my shop."

"Will you trade?" Grace asked the woman.

"As if you have anything worth trading!" the woman said with a laugh. "But yes, I trade."

Grace looked around the shop. The crowded room was full of every kind of thing. Pictures and mirrors leaned against the walls. Shelves were lined with plates and candlesticks. On a mantel stood five different clocks. Differently shaped glasses filled two bookcases. What could Grace have that this woman would want?

Then Grace saw a table behind the counter lined with dolls. They were porcelain dolls, like hers, like Penny.

"Time to be going," the woman said sharply.

"Please don't sell the china gentleman," Grace said as she went to the door. "I think I have something to trade. I'll be back. Please don't let anyone else have him."

"I can't promise anything," the woman said. "Close the door tight when you leave."

Grace hurried home. She barely saw where she was going, she was thinking so hard. She let herself into the apartment and ran straight to the bedroom. There was Penny, sitting on the small dresser top, waiting for her. The doll's dress looked

Grace saw a table lined with dolls. "I think I have
something to trade," she said, and hurried home.

more worn and faded than ever. Grace took Penny into her arms and sat on the bed with her.

"You'd forgive me, wouldn't you?" Grace whispered. She stroked the doll's porcelain face, as if wiping away tears. "It would be for Mama."

Grace looked into Penny's eyes, and the doll's calm gaze seemed to reassure Grace of something. It would be so hard to give her up. But she would do it, if it might make Mama happy.

It was dark outside now, and Mama would be home soon. Grace decided she would return to the curio shop with Penny the next day. She went to the sink and gently washed Penny's face with a dishcloth. Then she put her back in her place on the dresser for the night.

The next morning, Grace watched her mother carefully. She wondered if Mama could guess what she planned to do. Grace had never kept an important secret from her mother before. But it would all be worth it come Christmas Eve, when they had always given each other presents, only this day and one night away.

When her mother was at the sink, Grace slipped into the bedroom. She put on

"You'd forgive me, wouldn't you?"

her coat and tucked Penny into the front. She buttoned her coat to the top, her fin=gers fumbling. Then she rushed to the door. "Bye, Mama," she called. "Francie and Millicent are waiting for me."

"Yes? Well, all right, Grace," her mother answered. "I'll see you tonight."

Grace went into the hall. Then she realized she had forgotten to kiss her mother good=bye. She turned back and quickly kissed Mama's cheek. Then she ran down the steps to the street.

All day at school, Grace thought about the china gentleman, and whether the woman at the curio shop would let her trade Penny for the china gentleman. She put Penny in her desk, and every time she opened the top to reach for another book or a pencil, the doll's gentle gaze met hers. "It's for Mama," she would say to her=self. "It's for Mama."

At last the final bell rang. Grace pulled on her coat and ran from the school before her friends could find her. She hurried down one street after another until she was in front of the curio shop. She looked in the picture window for the china gentleman. He wasn't there.

"It's for Mama," she said to herself. "It's for Mama."

Grace pushed open the door to the shop. "Is he gone?" she cried to the woman, who stood behind the counter just as she had the day before.

"No children allowed!" snapped the woman.

"But the china gentleman," Grace said. "I asked you not to let him go. Is he gone?"

"Oh, it's you," the woman said, only a bit less sharply. "It's right over here." She came out from behind the counter and took the figurine from the top of a bookcase. "It still costs five dollars."

"I've brought something to trade," Grace said.

The woman laughed. "Oh yes, that's right. Well, what is it?"

"I have my doll." Grace pulled Penny out from the front of her coat and tried to smooth her crumpled dress.

"Indeed!" the woman cried, suddenly smiling. "Let me take a look."

The woman took Penny from Grace and examined the doll's porcelain face closely. "No cracks," she said. She looked at each of the arms and legs and tugged at the coppery hair. "Yes, this is worth something," she mumbled to herself. Then she said to Grace, "The dress is in terrible shape. That brings down the value."

"Indeed!" the woman cried. "Let me take a look."

"Her dress got dirty," Grace said, "but I washed it myself. With soap."

"Cheap lye soap, no doubt," the woman snapped. "The dress is ruined. But the doll itself is in good condition."

"So you will let me trade her for the china gentleman?" Grace asked.

"Well," the woman said, looking over the tops of her glasses at Grace, "I don't know if that's a fair trade. A fine figurine like that for a half-ruined doll?"

"It's all I have," Grace said.

"All right." The woman tucked the doll away under the counter. "Even a doll in this condition will sell in no time so close to Christmas. Otherwise, I wouldn't allow the trade. You understand that, don't you?"

Grace nodded, biting her lip so she wouldn't cry. She closed her eyes. "Good-bye, Penny," she whispered to herself.

The woman wrapped the figurine in a crumpled piece of brown paper and tied it with a piece of string. She handed the package to Grace. "It's yours. The 'china gentleman,' as you call it."

"Thank you," Grace whispered. She carefully tucked the bundle into the top of her coat. As she opened the door of the shop, the woman called to her.

"Now don't think you can change your mind and come back," she said.

"No, I understand," Grace said. She hugged the package close under her coat and shut the door behind her.

Grace hurried through the streets toward home. She tried not to think about Penny, that she would never see her again. She wanted to cry. But at the same time she could hardly believe that she carried in her coat the most perfect Christmas gift for Mama.

☆　☆　☆　☆　☆

As soon as Grace got upstairs, she went into the bedroom and unwrapped the china figure, just to make sure he was safe, and real. Suddenly she heard a key in the door — Mama was home! Quickly she wrapped up the china gentleman again and tucked him into her drawer.

That evening, Grace could hardly keep still, she was so excited. Mama seemed happy, too, as she warmed up a supper of thick soup and bread and put out the plates.

"What did you do today, Grace?" she asked, a new brightness in her voice.

"It was our last day at school before the Christmas holiday," Grace said. "But we still did all our lessons." Grace didn't want to talk about what she had done after school.

"Well, no more lessons for now," Mama said. "Tomorrow is Christmas Eve, and we'll open gifts then, just as we always did."

Grace's heart leapt up. "Yes!" she said. How glad she was that she had this gift for Mama!

That night, as they got ready to go to bed, Mama paused in front of the dresser. "Have you decided to keep Penny in a new place?" she asked.

Grace felt her face flush suddenly. "Oh, I've put her someplace else. Let's read a story, Mama," she said quickly. "A Christmas story, to make Christmas Eve come sooner."

"What a grand idea!" Mama said with a laugh, and she climbed onto the bed with Grace.

When Grace awoke in the morning, Mama was up already, hanging paper chains in the other room.

"A Christmas story, to make Christmas Eve come sooner."

"We won't have a Christmas tree this year," Mama said, "but we can still be festive."

"Yes, let's be festive!" Grace said. She hadn't seen Mama so happy in a very long time.

Grace quickly ate the biscuits Mama had kept warm for her in the oven. Then she helped Mama cut red and green paper into strips and loop them together into more chains. They sang Christmas carols, "We Three Kings" and "Silent Night" and "Joy to the World." Grace was filled with happiness, hearing her mother's sweet voice singing again and thinking of her gift for Mama.

Finally, they looped all their strips together into one long chain. They got up on the chairs to hang it across the windows. Grace stood on tip=toe to hook her end of the chain onto the curtain rod. And then she noticed the small shelf between the windows. It was empty. The china lady was gone.

"Mama!" Grace cried, jumping from her chair. "The china lady — where is she?"

"Why, I had to bring her someplace," her mother said.

Grace was filled with happiness thinking of her gift for Mama.

"She didn't — she didn't break, did she?" Grace asked.

"No, she's not broken," Mama said. She stepped down from her chair and kissed Grace on the forehead. "Grace," she said, "I'd like to give you your Christmas gift now, instead of waiting till evening. How about that?"

"All right, Mama," Grace whispered. She sat down on the old sofa while her mother reached for something in the closet. Mama sat beside her and placed in her hands a small bundle wrapped in cloth. "Merry Christmas, Grace," she said.

Grace pulled at the scrap tied around the bundle and unwrapped the cloth. Inside was another bundle of white, lacy cloth. She unfolded this bundle. It was a small, beautiful dress, just the right size for a porcelain doll.

"Oh, Mama!" Grace said softly.

"I've seen how you care for Penny, washing her things and trying to take good care of her," Mama said. "I wanted to sew the dress myself, but I couldn't learn fast enough. So I promised the china figurine to Mrs. Reedy, the seamstress at the shop, and in exchange she sewed the dress for me. So, you see, that's where the china lady has gone."

"Oh, Mama," Grace said again. "It's beautiful." She stroked the delicate white dress and tried not to cry. At last, Grace put her arms around her mother. "I have a gift for you, too."

Grace ran into the bedroom and pulled the paper=wrapped package out from her drawer.

"Merry Christmas, Mama," she said, as she stood before her.

"Thank you, Grace," Mama said, "but don't you want to bring Penny in here?"

"No, Mama, please just open your present," Grace said.

Mama looked at Grace strangely. "All right," she said. She untied the string and unwrapped the paper, and in a moment she held the china gentleman in her hands.

"Oh, Grace!" Mama said softly. "Where did you ever find this?"

"I saw him in a shop," Grace said. "I wanted you to have him, so that the china lady wouldn't have to dance alone. I wanted to give you the most perfect Christmas gift, and so I traded Penny for the china gentleman."

Mama was silent for a moment. She looked at Grace as if she hadn't seen her in a very long time. Then she pulled her onto her lap and hugged her tightly. "My little Grace!" she cried. "You have given me the most perfect gift."

Grace started to cry, and her mother held her. "But the china lady is still all alone," Grace said, her voice muffled with tears.

"She's not alone, Grace," Mama said, smoothing Grace's hair with her fingers.

"We're not alone. I've been missing Papa so much that I had almost forgotten

"You have given me the most perfect gift."

the most important thing. We have each other. And we'll always have Papa, too, in our hearts. We're not ever alone, as long as we have our love."

After a while, Mama took out her handkerchief and dried Grace's face.

"Shall we have a Christmas dance?" she asked. "I remember we promised you that last year."

Grace nodded and smiled.

Mama offered her hands to Grace. Grace took them, and together they rose. Mama tapped her foot and began to hum a melody from the "Blue Danube Waltz." And together they danced and swirled around the room as the china gentleman looked on.

Together they danced, as the china gentleman looked on.

AUTHOR'S NOTE

This story was inspired by "The Gift of the Magi," by O. Henry, which I first read when I was ten years old. O. Henry's story still moves me as more than an ironic tale of the unintended results of well=intentioned gifts. It is an ode to the ultimate value not of presents but of presence, not of gifts but of the heart that gives all.